'Twas the DAY before CHRISTMAS

The Story of
Clement Clarke Moore's
Beloved Poem

Brenda Seabrooke
illustrated by Delana Bettoli

Dutton Children's Books

To Kerria, Kevin, and Ian,
who make Christmas sparkle,
and to my editor,
Rosanne Lauer

B.S.

For my brother, Steven Bettoli,
and his love of the details
in early America

D.B.

DUTTON CHILDREN'S BOOKS
A division of Penguin Young Readers Group

Published by the Penguin Group
Penguin Group (USA) Inc., 375 Hudson Street, New York, New York 10014, U.S.A. ✦ Penguin Group (Canada), 90 Eglinton Avenue East, Suite 700, Toronto,
Ontario, Canada M4P 2Y3 (a division of Pearson Penguin Canada Inc.) ✦ Penguin Books Ltd, 80 Strand, London WC2R 0RL, England ✦ Penguin Ireland, 25 St
Stephen's Green, Dublin 2, Ireland (a division of Penguin Books Ltd) ✦ Penguin Group (Australia), 250 Camberwell Road, Camberwell, Victoria 3124, Australia
(a division of Pearson Australia Group Pty Ltd) ✦ Penguin Books India Pvt Ltd, 11 Community Centre, Panchsheel Park, New Delhi - 110 017, India ✦ Penguin
Group (NZ), 67 Apollo Drive, Rosedale, North Shore 0632, New Zealand (a division of Pearson New Zealand Ltd) ✦ Penguin Books (South Africa) (Pty) Ltd,
24 Sturdee Avenue, Rosebank, Johannesburg 2196, South Africa Penguin Books Ltd, Registered Offices: 80 Strand, London WC2R 0RL, England

Text copyright © 2008 by Brenda Seabrooke
Illustrations copyright © 2008 by Delana Bettoli
All rights reserved.

CIP Data is available.

Published in the United States by Dutton Children's Books,
a division of Penguin Young Readers Group
345 Hudson Street, New York, New York 10014
www.penguin.com/youngreaders

Designed by Sara Reynolds and Abby Kuperstock
Manufactured in China ✦ First Edition
ISBN 978-0-525-47816-4
1 3 5 7 9 10 8 6 4 2

On Christmas Eve afternoon in 1822, Clement Clarke Moore, bundled up against the frosty outdoors, waited in the hall for his sleigh. His wife, Eliza, had asked him to go to the market to buy one more turkey. She wanted to be sure they would have enough for all their family and guests coming for Christmas dinner. His daughter Charity tiptoed into the hall and tugged at his coat.

"Did you write it yet, Papa?" she whispered.

Clement smiled and put his finger to his lips. "It will be ready tonight," he said. "Remember, this is our secret."

"I won't tell," Charity said.

December 24th 1822

At the sound of the sleigh bells his other children—Margaret, carrying baby Emily, Mary, Benjamin, and Clement, Jr.—ran into the hall to see him off.

"Hurry back, Papa," they called as he stepped out into the cold air and climbed into the sleigh. He turned to wave and reassure them that he would be back long before time for Saint Nick's visit.

Patrick, his driver, whistled to the team of horses, and the sleigh glided down the snowy lane, sounding a merry jingle.

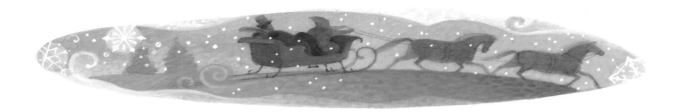

Clement sat back in the sleigh to think about what he had promised Charity: to write a special surprise for his children for Christmas. He wouldn't have much time when he got home. Washington Market was almost at the tip of Manhattan Island in the city of New York. By the time he got back, his children would be anxious to hang their stockings for Saint Nicholas's visit.

The children loved their papa's stories. At bedtime, they would gather around the fireside to hear about when Papa was a boy, about George Washington visiting his grandmother, and tales from his reading.

While thinking about the gift for his children, he had read his friend Washington Irving's account of Christmas when New York was a Dutch colony, called New Amsterdam, in Irving's *Knickerbocker Tales*.

Clement and Eliza were both descended from the first settlers of New Amsterdam. The Moores had always celebrated Christmas in the Dutch way, though now they hung stockings for Saint Nicholas to fill instead of putting out wooden shoes.

Clement had also read about Saint Nicholas himself, a Turkish bishop who befriended children. Clement's own father, Benjamin Moore, had been a bishop, too, the Episcopal bishop of New York. Clement thought about his father. Christmas had always been his favorite holiday, the happiest time of the year, when friends and family came together at Chelsea, the one-hundred-acre farm where Clement now lived in the big old house with his own family.

Clement wanted to write something that would bring the joy and wonder of those childhood Christmases to his children.

Now that he knew what he wanted to write about, Clement had to decide in what form to write it. Should he write a story or a poem? Sometimes he wrote funny rhyming verse for his family, like the one about a lazy pig. Last year he had read a poem in *The Children's Friend* magazine. Clement tried to remember how it went. "Old Santeclause with much delight/His reindeer drives this frosty night." The rhythm didn't sound right to Clement. He felt the urge to write in his fingertips, but he still didn't know quite what to say.

The sleigh turned out of the gates of Chelsea onto the North-South Road, across on Roy Road onto Love Lane and then to Greenwich Street for the almost four-mile trip.

Last night's new-fallen snow spread over fields and farms and flocked the bare trees in the orchards, still called bouweries from the Old Dutch. Snow crystals sparkled like diamonds in the late-afternoon sun.

They met a few other sleighs in the village of Greenwich, passing St. Luke's, the Moores' church. Snow drifted against houses, blanketed rooftops, pillowed below windows wreathed with frost and greenery.

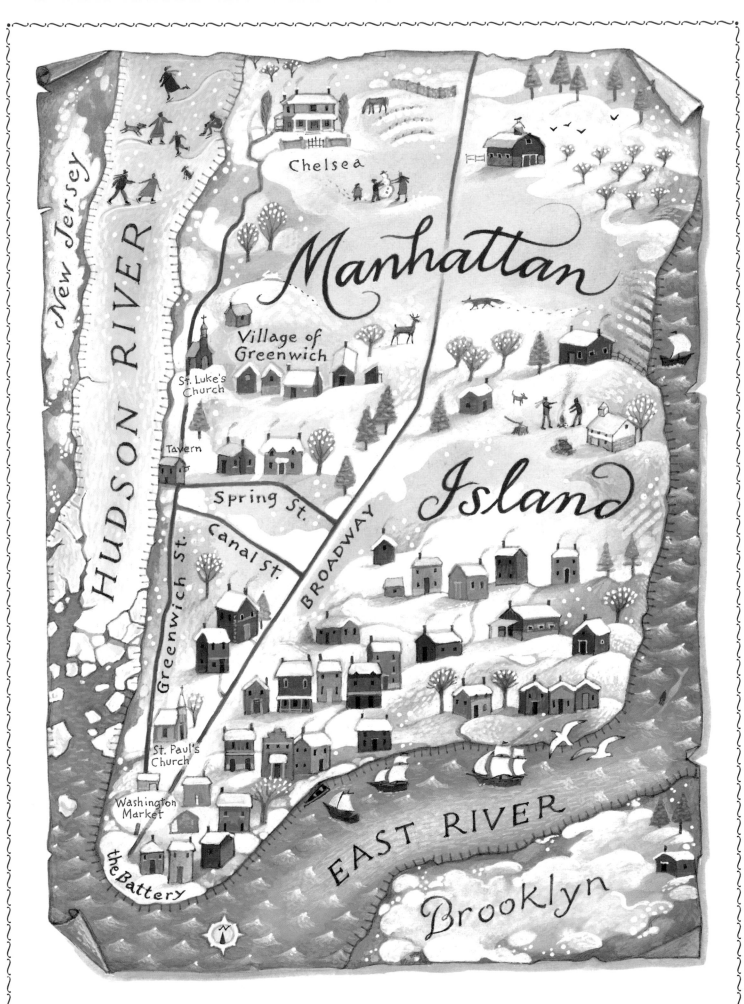

This was the coldest winter in New York that anyone remembered. The Hudson River had frozen all the way across to New Jersey. Skaters swooped and spun on the ice. Children frolicked in the snow as they counted the hours before Saint Nick's visit.

Patrick kept the horses on a steady course in the lane, through a countryside that was white as far as the eye could see.

Clement thought of his children waiting at home anticipating the joys of Christmas—Margaret, seven; Charity, six; Benjamin, four; Mary, three; Clement, Jr., two; and little Emily, only one, but excited because her brothers and sisters were. Charity was counting on her papa to write the surprise. How could he make Christmas real for his children?

As the sleigh approached the thickly settled area of New York, traffic picked up and the air rang with sleigh bells and song. *"Good King Wenceslas looked out,"* sang carolers on street corners. Crowds gathered to listen and give them pennies.

"Hot tea! Hot gingerbread! Sugarplums! Roasted chestnuts!" called the street vendors.

Patrick turned the sleigh onto Vesey Street, two blocks behind St. Paul's Chapel on Broadway. The open-air Washington Market stretched for several blocks to the Hudson River and teemed with last-minute shoppers like Clement.

Patrick stayed with the horses while Clement walked quickly past stalls selling fish, fruit, and vegetables. "Fresh oysters!" called the seller from his stall, where all manner of seafood was displayed. Clement was tempted, but Eliza had said to get only a turkey, and that was all he had time to buy. He hurried to the turkey stall and picked out a plump one that would probably be enough for all their guests even without the hams, mince pies, the turkey they already had, and all the other food being prepared. This turkey would certainly please Eliza.

Standing by a vendor's fire warming his hands, Patrick sprang to help Clement with his bundle when he returned. Clement climbed in the sleigh and settled down to think during the long ride home. Patrick picked up the reins and whistled to the team. "On, Dasher! On, Dancer!"

As they left the market, lamplighters were lighting the whale-oil lamps. The deep snow was almost blue in the gathering dusk. Lanterns and candles twinkled like distant stars in the scattered houses. Some farmers went to bed at dusk, even on Christmas Eve. A man already in his nightcap looked out the window as the sleigh passed his house. Maybe he thought it was Saint Nick already! The man's children probably hoped it was.

Clement wished the sleigh could go faster, that it could fly over the housetops like the balloon he had seen go up when he was ten. He remembered how magical the balloon had seemed flying through the air.

They hardly passed any houses between the tavern at Spring Street and St. Luke's in Greenwich. Nothing moved over the silent fields beyond as Clement listened to the music of the harness bells and the rhythmic *clop, clop, clop, clop* of the horses' hooves on the snow-packed lane.

It is Christmas Eve. No, *'twas the night before Christmas.* Words danced through Clement's head to the rhythm of the horses. *'Twas the night before Christmas.* His thoughts were ready to be written. He had the beginning, but to what? A story? A poem?

Clement could tell a story in the twinkling of an eye. But he had promised Charity a special treat: poems were harder, but rhymes delighted his children. Surely the horses' hooves were telling him something. What was the night before Christmas like when he was a boy? What was it like for his children? They would go to bed excited, dreaming of their favorite things, like sugarplums. *'Twas the night before Christmas when all through the house . . . children were excited.* No, that was telling. He wanted his children to feel the excitement of Christmas, not have it described to them.

Night had almost fallen over Chelsea when Patrick drove through the gates. Lantern and candlelight spilled onto the snow to welcome Clement home. As he stepped from the sleigh, he looked at Patrick, and words jumped into his head: . . . *a little old driver, so lively and quick.* Patrick's cheeks were ruddy from the cold as Clement thanked him for the smooth, safe journey.

Piet, the old Dutch handyman, came to help. His beard was as white as the snow surrounding the house. He was bundled against the cold, but his nose was as red as his cap. He slung the bag with the turkey over his shoulder, and Clement thought of Saint Nick with his pack.

Charity met him eagerly at the door. "I didn't tell, Papa," she said. "I was as quiet as a mouse."

Clement winked at her as he went into his study. He sat down at his desk. Through the window, the moon shone on the fresh snow and made the world seem bright as day. He picked up a quill pen. Now his thoughts came as thick as snowflakes. He dipped the quill into a bottle of ink and began to write. *'Twas the night before Christmas, when all through the house, not a creature was stirring not even a . . .* What wasn't stirring on the night before Christmas? A child? It didn't sound right.

For the moment the Moore house was quiet. It usually wasn't so with so many children about. It was quiet enough to hear the clock tick. Or a mouse squeak.

He had to hurry to finish in time to read his gift to his children before their bedtime. His pen flew across the page, ending with *And away they all flew*. But it needed something more. Clement thought of his father. He had always wished his family good-night before bedtime. And he had always wished his friends Happy Christmas. Clement dipped the quill one more time.

He put the finishing touches on the poem just in time for supper. The family sat down at the table, but the children were almost too excited to eat, waiting for Saint Nick. Charity kept looking at her papa for a sign that the treat was ready. When no one was looking, he winked at her to let her know it was.

The meal seemed to last forever, but finally they finished and gathered around the hearth in the parlor. The room glowed with light from the hearth fire and candles and was scented with the fragrance of wreaths and swags of greenery. Clement looked around at his family —his mother, Charity Clarke Moore; his wife, Eliza; and their children.

"Now, Papa? Now can we have our treat?" Charity asked. "Papa promised me he would write a surprise for us for Christmas," she told her brothers and sisters.

"A treat!" Mary clapped her hands.

"Is it a story?" Benjamin asked.

"What is it about?" asked Margaret.

Clement took out the copy of the poem that told a story. He hardly had to look at it. The words seemed to be printed in his heart. He cleared his throat and read—

A Visit from Saint Nicholas

'Twas the night before Christmas, when all through the house,
not a creature was stirring, not even a mouse.

The stockings were hung by the chimney with care,
in hopes that Saint Nicholas soon would be there.

The children were nestled all snug in their beds,
while visions of sugarplums danced in their heads;

And Mamma in her kerchief, and I in my cap,
had just settled our brains for a long winter's nap—

when out on the lawn there arose such a clatter,
I sprang from my bed to see what was the matter.
Away to the window I flew like a flash,
tore open the shutter, and threw up the sash.

The moon on the breast of the new-fallen snow
gave a luster of midday to objects below;
when, what to my wondering eyes should appear,
but a miniature sleigh and eight tiny reindeer,
With a little old driver, so lively and quick,
I knew in a moment it must be Saint Nick!

More rapid than eagles his coursers they came,
and he whistled and shouted and called them by name.
"Now, Dasher, Now, Dancer! Now, Prancer and Vixen!
On, Comet! On, Cupid! On, Donder and Blitzen!
To the top of the porch, to the top of the wall,
now, dash away, dash away, dash away all!"
As dry leaves that before the wild hurricane fly,
when they meet with an obstacle, mount to the sky,
so, up to the housetop the coursers they flew,
with a sleigh full of toys—and Saint Nicholas, too.

And then, in a twinkling, I heard on the roof
the prancing and pawing of each little hoof.

As I drew in my head and was turning around,
down the chimney Saint Nicholas came with a bound.

He was dressed all in fur from his head to his foot,
and his clothes were all tarnished with ashes and soot:
A bundle of toys he had flung on his back,
and he looked like a peddler just opening his pack.

His eyes, how they twinkled! His dimples, how merry!

His cheeks were like roses, his nose like a cherry.

His droll little mouth was drawn up like a bow,

And the beard on his chin was as white as the snow.

The stump of his pipe he held tight in his teeth,

and the smoke, it encircled his head like a wreath.

He had a broad face and a little round belly

that shook when he laughed like a bowl full of jelly.

He was chubby and plump, a right jolly old elf,

and I laughed when I saw him, in spite of myself.

A wink of his eye, and a twist of his head,

soon gave me to know I had nothing to dread.

He spoke not a word, but went straight to his work,

and filled all the stockings: then turned with a jerk,

and laying his finger aside of his nose,

and giving a nod, up the chimney he rose.

He sprang to his sleigh, to his team gave a whistle,

and away they all flew like the down on a thistle.

But I heard him exclaim, ere they drove out of sight,

"Happy Christmas to all, and to all a good-night!"

Clement looked up. No one said a word. His family sat in silence. He waited for someone to speak, to say something. Hadn't they liked it? The children were staring at him. Charity's mouth made an *O*. What was the matter? The poem couldn't be that bad, could it?

He looked at Eliza. Her eyes were shining. Were those tears? His mother's, too?

And then the children erupted, clambering all over him, shouting their favorite lines.

"'The prancing and pawing of each little hoof.'"

"'And his clothes were all tarnished with ashes and soot.' From the chimneys, Papa?"

"He looked like a peddler, Papa! Like the peddler who came last summer?"

"Shubberpums! Shubberpums!" shouted Clement, Jr., around his thumb.

"Read it again, Papa," they begged.

Clement read the poem again. The children pleaded for a third reading and then a fourth, but it was long past their bedtime. He reminded them it was still Christmas Eve. Saint Nicholas would soon be there.

The children hung their stockings and went to bed, whispering lines
from the poem.

"Happy Christmas to all, and to all a good-night!"

Charity lingered behind the others.

"Thank you, Papa," she said, hugging him.

"Thank you, Papa," Clement whispered later when he was alone and thinking of his own father, who had given him the happy gift of Christmas.

On Christmas morning the stockings brimmed with sugarplums and toys, while other presents too big for the stockings sat on the floor. But all of Clement's children said that the best present was the poem. And *that* was the best present they could give their father. To know that he had brought happiness to his family was the greatest gift to Clement Clarke Moore.

He did not know then that he had also given the world a gift for the ages—the poem that on Christmas Eve fills the minds and hearts of children the world over with the magical wonder of Jolly Saint Nicholas.